I Can't Catch That Fish!

(He's My Friend, Don't You See?)

Elena Schietinger

Illustrated by Michael C. Perez

Archway Publishing books may be ordered through booksellers or by contacting:

Archway Publishing
1663 Liberty Drive
Bloomington, IN 47403
www.archwaypublishing.com
844-669-3957

Interior Image Credit: Michael C. Perez

ISBN: 978-1-6657-4072-2 (sc)
ISBN: 978-1-6657-4071-5 (hc)
ISBN: 978-1-6657-4073-9 (e)

Print information available on the last page.

Archway Publishing rev. date: 08/16/2023

This book is dedicated to Kenny,
my forever favorite fisher!

One day while out fishing
in the river so deep,
a friendly little fish
swam around at my feet.

2

4

It swam and it swam,
and all I could see
was that friendly little fish
that kept following me.

I walked to the left,
and the fish was right there
swimming around
without even a care.

6

I moved to the right,
and guess what he did?
Next to my leg
he swiftly then slid.

7

As I kept on with fishing
the little fish stayed
though all of his friends
seemed to have strayed.

8

That fish sure did like me!
He'd found a new friend,
right there in the water
where the river did bend.

All day it continued.
The sun started to set.
The little fish near me
was all I had met.

Then along came a fisher,
and the fisher said to me,
"How many did you catch?
Come here, let me see."

"I haven't caught any,"
I said as I sighed.
"Trust me, oh trust me,
I tried and I tried."

The fisher looked down
and saw at my feet
the little fish swimming,
that fish I did meet.

"I can't catch that fish!"
I told the old man.
"That fish is my friend.
He's not part of the plan."

18

I looked at the fish
and the fish looked at me
and I knew that forever
my friend he would be.

20

"I don't want a fish
that bad," I did say.
"I'd rather just wait
and try another day."

22

So the man walked away
as the sun slowly set
and I smiled as I looked down
at the friend I had met.

Other books by Elena Schietinger:

There's A Spider In My Closet!
I Know You Can Do It, You Know You Can, Too!
How The Goldfish Got Its Name
Hello, It's Me!
The No Snow North Pole

Printed in the United States
by Baker & Taylor Publisher Services